Max's Christmas

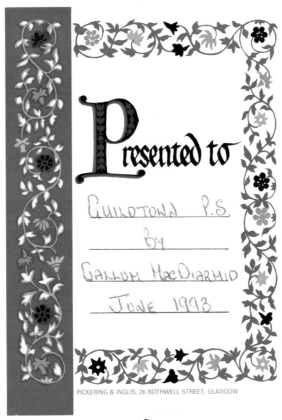

$\mathcal{P}$resented to

Guildtown P.S.

By

Callum MacDiarmid

June 1993

PICKERING & INGLIS, 26 BOTHWELL STREET, GLASGOW

For Beezoo Wells

First published in the USA by
Dial Books for Young Readers,
a Division of NAL Penguin Inc in 1986
First published in Great Britain by
William Collins Sons & Co Ltd in 1986
First published in Picture Lions in 1988
This edition published in 1992

Picture Lions is an imprint of the Children's Division,
part of HarperCollins Publishers Limited,
77-85 Fulham Palace Road, Hammersmith,
London W6 8JB

ISBN: 0 00 663325-0

Printed in Great Britain

Max's Christmas

ROSEMARY WELLS

PictureLions

An Imprint of HarperCollins*Publishers*

Guess what, Max!
said Max's sister Ruby.
What? said Max.

It's Christmas Eve, Max, said Ruby,
and you know who's coming!
Who? said Max.

Santa Claus is coming,
that's who, said Ruby.
When? said Max.

Tonight, Max, he's coming tonight!
said Ruby.
Where? said Max.
Spit, Max, said Ruby.

Santa Claus is coming right down
our chimney into our living room,
said Ruby.
How? said Max.

That's enough questions, Max.

You have to go to sleep fast,
before Santa Claus comes, said Ruby.

But Max wanted to stay up
to see Santa Claus.
No, Max, said Ruby.

Nobody ever sees Santa Claus.
Why? said Max.
BECAUSE! said Ruby.

But Max didn't believe a word
Ruby said.

So he sneaked downstairs...

and waited for Santa Claus.

Max waited a long time.

Suddenly, ZOOM! Santa
jumped down the chimney
into the living room.

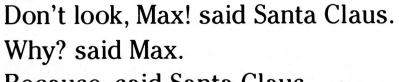

Don't look, Max! said Santa Claus.
Why? said Max.
Because, said Santa Claus,
nobody is supposed to see me!

Why? said Max.
Because everyone is supposed to be asleep in bed, said Santa Claus.

But Max peeked at Santa anyway.
Guess what, Max! said Santa Claus.
What? said Max.

It's time for me to go away
and you to go to sleep,
said Santa Claus.
Why? said Max.

BECAUSE! said Santa Claus.

Ruby came downstairs.
What happened, Max? asked Ruby.
Who were you talking to?
Where did you get that hat?

BECAUSE! said Max.

Here are some more Picture Lions for you to enjoy

ALPACA   *Rosemary Billam & Vanessa Julian-Ottie*
MR MAGNOLIA   *Quentin Blake*
THE WINTER BEAR   *Ruth Craft*
KATIE MORAG DELIVERS THE MAIL   *Mairi Hedderwick*
THE MOST WONDERFUL EGG IN THE WORLD   *Helme Heine*
ALFIE GETS IN FIRST   *Shirley Hughes*
MOG, THE FORGETFUL CAT   *Judith Kerr*
MAISIE MIDDLETON   *Nita Sowter*
NOISY NORA   *Rosemary Wells*
STANLEY AND RHODA   *Rosemary Wells*